BIG RAIN COMING

For all the wonderful kids at Minyerri
Love Katrina xo

To Jack and Ella — BB

Clarion Books
a Houghton Mifflin Company imprint
215 Park Avenue South, New York, NY 10003
Text copyright © 1999 by Katrina Germein
Illustrations copyright © 1999 by Bronwyn Bancroft

First published in Australia in 1999 by Roland Harvey Books,
Level 1 /1 Bleakhouse Lane, Albert Park, Victoria 3207.
Roland Harvey Books is an imprint of Roland Harvey Studios.

Designed by Petrina Griffin

Illustrations executed in gouache and acrylic canvas paint.

Printed in China by Everbest Printing Co., Ltd.

Library of Congress Cataloging-in-Publication Data

Germein, Katrina.
Big rain coming / by Katrina Germein ; illustrated by Bronwyn Bancroft.
p. cm.
Summary: Though everyone eagerly awaits the rain, it is slow in coming.

[1. Rain and rainfall--Fiction. 2. Patience--Fiction. 3. Australia--Fiction.] I. Bancroft, Bronwyn, ill. II.

PZ7.G299 Bi 2000
[Fic]--dc21

00-022914

ISBN 0-618-08344-8

10 9 8 7 6 5 4 3 2 1

billabong: water hole

the Rainbow Serpent, depicted at the bottom of most
pages in this book: a symbol of creation in the Dreamtime
(in the Aboriginal belief system, a collection of events
beyond living memory that shaped the physical, spiritual,
and moral world). Associated with water and life,
the Rainbow Serpent is seen as fashioning the earth
and connecting the land with everyone and everything in it.

BIG RAIN COMING

COMING

Katrina Germein

Illustrated by Bronwyn Bancroft

Clarion Books · New York

On Sunday afternoon
Old Stephen nodded to
the dark clouds spreading
in the south.

"Big rain coming," he said.

But on Monday there was no rain.

The night was so warm Rosie's kids dragged their beds outside

On Tuesday, there was still no rain.

The panting dogs at Roberta's place dug themselves

dusty holes to keep cool.

Wednesday came, and still no rain.

The children swam in the billabong after school.

The water was warm and still.

By Thursday night there was still no rain.

The fat green frogs

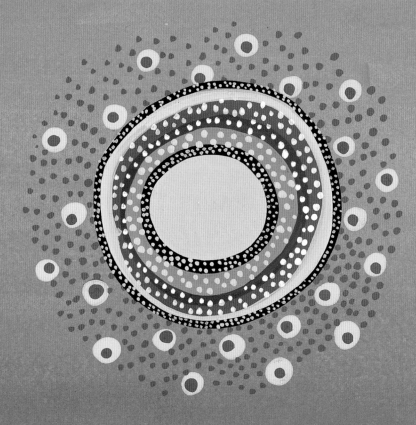

huddled around the leaky tap on the rainwater tank.

Then on Friday evening
the thick gray clouds
over the hills were echoing
with thunder.

"Big rain coming," said Stephen.

But there was still no rain.

On Saturday, there was rain.

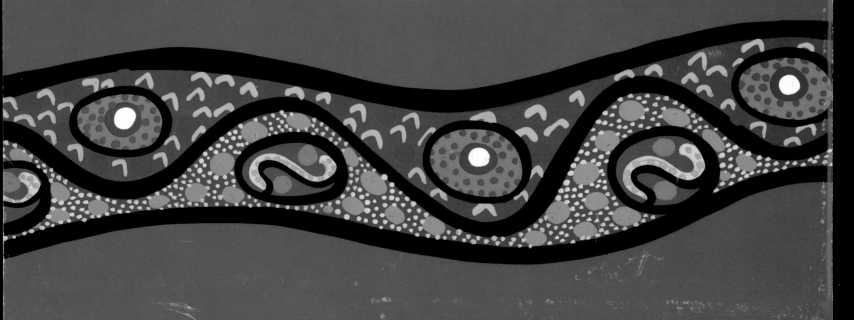